BULLDOG

HEARTLANDS MC

HOPE FORD

Editor: Kasi Alexander

Photographer: Regina Wamba

Cover Design: Cormar Covers

www.authorhopeford.com

1

KATE

Forty. The big four o. It happened a few weeks ago, and I have to admit it's been an adjustment. It wasn't like I didn't see it coming. I just didn't think turning forty was going to give me even a moment's pause. Instead it gave me a smack in the face stop sign. It was like I suddenly realized I needed to stop and look around and evaluate how my life is going. The time had passed where I could say I'd get around to doing things I wanted to do later. Because later is now.

Having lived my life very carefully and responsibly makes me realize that maybe I should have taken advantage of my younger years a bit more. Had some fun, lived a little dangerously. Instead, I did what I thought was expected of me. Graduated high school, went to college, and graduated with a business degree. Started a career. Got married. Had a child. I did everything I thought I was supposed to do. And then it all seemed to start falling apart.

I try to pinpoint exactly when I started feeling restless, but there's not specifically one event that caused it. Most people would think that discovering my husband of fifteen years was sleeping around was it. But it wasn't. Staying in the marriage was more for my husband saving face than anything. It didn't destroy me, heck it was more of a relief than anything when I found out about his indiscretions. What I thought was my duty, to stay married, went to the wayside when I found out about his infidelity.

So the only thing I can attribute to my wanting more is everything, all of it. I'm forty, single, and looking for something. I just don't know what yet.

Luckily, my friends from work seem to understand that I'm going through something. I've spent the last few years always turning down their invites to hang out together after work. So much to the point that they stopped asking. But today, when I am bemoaning my life, they invite me.

"Come with us on Friday," Tamara says to me and looks around the break room as if she's looking to see if anyone else is listening. I don't know why she bothers. It's only the four of us in here and it's our assigned lunch break. No one ever disrupts us. Which automatically makes me think she's about to invite me to a strip club.

No. Thank. You. Strip clubs are definitely not my scene. I'm already about to tell them no and Carrie leans over and snaps her finger in front of my face. "You said you needed something exciting. Well, this is exciting."

But I'm already shaking my head. "I'm not going to a strip club."

Bryce laughs. "Girl, I wish it was a strip club. Trust me if you've seen the men that go in there you would be wishing the same thing."

"Where?" I ask.

Bryce leans in and starts to whisper. "So, remember last week when I had my car in the shop? Well, it broke down close to that Heartlands Garage, and even though they primarily work on bikes, Maddox, one of the men that work there, offered to work on my car for me. Well, he was telling me about the Ride or Die Bar... and girl, we're going."

I lean back in my chair and start to laugh. I mean, I can't help it. I almost have to hold my stomach from laughing so hard. I look around the table at Bryce, Carrie, and Tamara. I'm the oldest of the bunch and feel like a mother to them more times than not. Sometimes, they get into some crazy stuff. "Not me, I'm not going to a bar called the Ride or Die. No way. No how."

Bryce leans over and grabs my arm. "Kate, it's a biker bar. And I mean the real deal. These guys are hard, handsome, tattooed." She does a big shivering motion with her shoulders. "Man, I can't even think about it without getting excited."

I laugh and pull my arm away from her clutches. "Calm down, girl. You're getting too excited for an accounting office. You may need to go down to the ladies in the marketing department if you keep this up."

"Har, har," she says. "I'm not joking, they are that hot." And she waves her hand in her face as if she's trying to cool herself off.

Well, if nothing else, lunch today is entertaining.

They spend the rest of our lunch break trying to convince me that I need to go, but I keep refusing. I've never been there, I don't even think I've driven by it, but I know it's not my thing.

The rest of the day goes by in a blur. I keep having this nagging feeling in the pit of my stomach. It's like I'm hyper aware that I need a change, I just don't know what that is. But I'm doing my best to ignore it.

My phone dings on my desk and I pick it up.

Ugh. A text from Charlie, my ex-husband.

Don't forget Friday night. I need you to help me host the dinner for the Seneca Bar Association.

My mouth drops and I start typing furiously. *We're not married. I'm not hosting anything.*

I almost text him to have his girlfriend, Chloe, help him, but by texting that it would imply I care that he has a girlfriend, which I do not.

I put my phone down and it dings again. I scan it quickly and type back, *I can't. I have plans.*

And before he can respond, I type out a group text to Tamara, Carrie, and Bryce. *I'm in. Ride or Die!*

I take a deep breath and push the send button. A few seconds go by and I hear a whoop from an office down the hall. Yep, pretty sure that was Tamara. Followed by laughter from Carrie and Bryce. They all chime in and my phone starts blowing up.

Yes!

Alright!

You are going to be glad you did!

I chuckle, send them all a heart emoji, and then I get back to work. But I still can't stop shaking my head. Who names their bar the Ride or Die? I mean, it seems pretty ominous to me.

My luck, it's probably a bunch of overweight, balding men that get together on weekends wishing they were real bikers. Regardless, it's probably not really dangerous, and it will be interesting if nothing else.

2

BULLDOG

Seventies rock is blaring from the ol' jukebox. It's a Friday night and the bar is already hopping and it's only nine o'clock. Working as the bouncer for the Ride or Die is never boring. There's always the same crew here, but it seems lately there's more and more outsiders showing up. It's a biker bar, after all, but tonight there's all kinds of people here.

Candace, a woman that comes in pretty regularly, has her arm on me and I know all I have to do is say the word. She'd go out with me- on a date, to the backroom, whatever I wanted. But just looking at her, I know she would be temporary and I'm starting to wish that the women in my life weren't so fleeting. It's not like they're wanting to exit my life. I'm the one with the walls up. It's just that the women I meet don't seem to have any substance to them. It seems that a lot of the guys of the Heartlands MC are settling down and I can't help but be a little jealous of what they've found. I've never seen them happier. But regardless, I know Candace is not what I want. So I dismiss her with a shrug of my head and then go back to looking at one table across the room.

I stare over at the four women that came in a little while ago. Well, actually I'm only looking at one of them. I don't know what it is that the women I've been kicking to the curb are missing exactly, but whatever it is, the woman that I can't seem to look away from has it. I knew when they came in they didn't belong here. I mean, they all dressed the part, well except for her. The beautiful redhead with the green eyes. She has on a long, fitted skirt and button-down shirt that is almost buttoned to the very top. The rest of the ladies have on short skirts and belly-baring shirts, and it's obvious they're looking for a good time. But my girl is sitting there, watching everything, and seems to be taking it all in. I wait for a look of disgust or even a lift of her nose, but she doesn't. She seems to just be observing it all.

I almost walk over to her table a dozen times, but for the first time in a long time I'm not quite sure how to approach her. I watch her with her friends, and it's obvious that she's the responsible one of the group, keeping track of her friends, and she's only been nursing a single beer for the past hour.

I nod at some friends coming in, slap knuckles and then look back at the table. My girl has her back to me now and she's watching her friend on the dance floor. Her friend has her skirt hiked high on her hips and she's swaying to the music. Right now, she's alone, but I know she won't be for long. I look around the bar and it seems she's giving a show. None of the men that are taken, Ranger, Saint, Jaxon, and Chain, are looking her way, but the rest of them are, and I know, like a nagging in my gut, that it's about to get bad.

I see the man get up from the bar and stagger over to her. At first she smiles at him, but when he gets handsy, she tries to pull away. I'm already making my way across the bar, but it seems the woman I had my eye on is going to beat me to it. She slides between her drunk friend and the man. Without even touching him, she somehow gets him to back down. I walk up in time to hear her say, "Sorry, but my friend's not interested."

The man just laughs and then looks my girl up and down. "What about you, honey? You interested?"

Before she can get a word out, I'm stepping up next to them, doing my best not to rip his eyes out for even looking at her. "No, she's not, John. Why don't you have a seat back at the bar?"

It seems my reputation proceeds me, and John doesn't even question me before turning to go. I barely watch him walk away before turning my back on him. I know he's not stupid enough to blindside me. Half the men in here would have him dragged out the back door before he got a second punch.

"Thank you," my girl says to me. I can't keep referring to her as my girl. A name. I need a name.

"You're welcome. But it looks like you had it under control before I got here," I compliment her.

She shrugs her shoulders and before she can turn away, I ask her, "What's your name?"

She tilts her head to the side but doesn't answer me immediately. I can tell she's weighing her thoughts before she decides to give in. But the heat is there. She's attracted to me, I can tell. Maybe it's because I want her, and it's hopeful thinking on my part, but I don't think so. The rapid beat of her pulse in her neck, the flare of her nostrils, and the way her eyes are darkening let me know she has some interest.

"Why do you want to know?" She finally answers me with her own question.

Her friend is looking between us and she seems to have sobered up, because her head is volleying back and forth easily, as if she doesn't want to miss a thing.

I could tell the little redhead that I want to know what I should be calling her when I'm driving my dick into her later, but she doesn't seem the type that would be impressed with that. So, instead, I'm honest with her. "Because I've been wondering since you walked in earlier. And I figure you're not ready for me to call you my girl like I have been doing in my head all night."

3

KATE

Oh, he's smooth. The sexy eye candy built to make women feel small and dainty, even thicker curvy girls like myself, is too much. For him to look and talk the way he does, he should definitely come with a warning label. Even though I managed to extract Carrie from the scary looking biker, I'm grateful to have an escort away from the guy who was looking to take full advantage of my too-drunk friend.

I meet his eyes and man, oh man, my body is already responding to him. He's young. Way too young for me, and I can't help but wonder if maybe he was hoping to save Carrie for himself. Maybe flirting with me to try and catch Carrie's eye? I look at Carrie and she's staring open-mouthed at him. I turn my head to look at our savior again, and he's still looking straight at me. "I'm Kate... and this is Carrie."

I don't wait for him to respond. I walk with Carrie over to the table with Bryce and Tamara. Carrie's on to me the whole way, telling me how handsome the guy was, and I was stupid to walk away. I don't even care. I don't feel as if I can breathe until I put some distance between us.

We no sooner get to the table than Carrie is telling Bryce and Tamara all about the man who had "goo goo" eyes for me. Her words, not mine.

I almost laugh at her antics until everyone in front of me gets really quiet and is staring behind me. I can feel him before he even says a thing.

I feel a warm hand on my shoulder, and I take a deep breath before I turn around. His hand slides across my shoulder, down my arm, and wraps around my fingers. "Dance with me... Kate."

I start to say no. I know I'm only going to look foolish. He's way too young, way too handsome, just way too much everything. But my friends aren't going to let me take the easy way out. Carrie puts her hands on my back and almost pushes me into his arms.

Luckily, he catches me, and I suck in a deep breath as I hit his hard chest. His big arms wrap around me, and I swear he almost carries me out to the dance floor. I pull back, but he still holds my hand the whole way. His scent surrounds me, woodsy and clean but also manly, and once he stops on the dance floor, he pulls me into his arms again.

I bite my lip and look for something to say. "You won't get in trouble, will you? For dancing? Are you supposed to be working?"

He shakes his head, and his stare is penetrating me. "No. I got Saint to cover the door. He can handle it."

I nod and ask him, "What's your name?"

"Bulldog," he answers and then grimaces, like he has a bad taste in his mouth. "But you can call me Bull."

One arm goes around my waist and fits me tighter against him. The way he takes charge on the dance floor, holding me like I've always been his, has my heart hammering in my chest, and I'm breathing fast, even though there's a slow song playing through the speakers. He's taller than me and bigger also. So I can ignore the fact that he's too young for me, as least right now, while we're dancing.

He pushes the hair off my face. "Where do you live?" As he speaks, his eyes stay focused on my lips.

I almost answer him, already wanting to give him everything he asks for. But common sense prevails. "Why do you want to know that?"

His hands slide up and down my back, and I loop my arms around his shoulders, my hands resting at the nape of his neck.

I swear as we sway, I can feel the bulge between his legs pressed against my belly. I start to look away, but he stops me. "I want to know so that after you drive your friends home I'll know where to meet you later."

My nipples tingle and his gruff, raspy voice sends chills down my body. I've never reacted like this to a man before, let alone one I just met. We're so close every time our bodies sway, I can feel his leg pressed between mine. I fight the urge to tighten my legs on his. He definitely knows what he's doing. "How old are you?"

He opens his mouth and then closes it.

I smile then, because I know he's young, but now I wonder just how young. I put my forehead on his chest and shake my head before I look up at him again. "Please tell me you're of legal age."

He laughs then and it's a hearty one that comes deep from his belly. "Twenty-four."

I slide my hands down from around his neck and grip his upper arms. I try to step away, but he's not having it. "Uh-uh, baby. Where do you think you're going?"

Like a hussy, I'm amazed by the feel of his arms flexing under my hands. Damn, he's hard, which makes me wonder if he's this hard everywhere. Shaking my head, I reach behind me to pry his hands off me, but when I do, he just grabs on to my hands and holds me. I'm sixteen years older than him. I keep waiting for him to ask me how old I am, but he doesn't.

As if he's afraid I'm going to walk away, he brings both my hands up to his chest and holds them there. His breath is hot on my face and it's like I can feel the emotion in his voice. "Fuck, I want to kiss you."

I should say no. I should tell him how old I am and then I know he'll let me walk away from him. But I don't. Staring into his eyes, I raise onto my tiptoes. He pulls one of my hands up to his shoulder, setting it there until I wrap it around the back of his neck.

He cups my face, still holding my other hand. He leans down and when his lips touch mine, I can feel the heat of it all the way to my toes.

He may be young, but he knows what he's doing. His tongue slides in and then out again. He's pushing me for more, the way he's angled his face and taking me in. His leg slides between mine, and I clench my legs on to him tightly because his kiss is already more than I can handle. I can't take much more.

When he pulls away, we're both gasping for breath, and I know I'm looking at him like he has a third eye or something, but sweet Mary, I've never been kissed like that before.

Finally, lifting from my daze, I realize that the reason he stopped was because of all the catcalls. The bikers are all laughing and making noise. I look back at my table of friends and all three of them are watching us with stunned looks on their faces.

I put my hands on his chest and push away from him, forcing myself to put some distance between us. But he doesn't let me go far. He holds his hand out to me. "Let me have your phone."

I don't even question him; I pull it out of my pocket and hand to him. As he types into it, he says, "I like it that you're being safe and not handing out your address. I'm going to text myself from your phone so I have your number."

It doesn't even register with me that maybe I shouldn't have given him my phone. I'm still too messed up and need to recover. He walks me back to the table before bending over and kissing my cheek. "Thanks for the dance... and the kiss."

4

KATE

The rest of the night is a blur. When he brought me back to the table, kissed me on the cheek, and walked away, I almost got up and followed him. But common sense prevailed. No matter how sexy he is, no matter how good the man can kiss, there's nothing that can come of it. My friends all go crazy and even call me cougar a few times, and even though I laugh, it still hurts a little.

I try to keep my eyes off him, but they keep straying over to the door where he's standing. And every time I look that way, he's staring right at me, and even across the room, I can see the heat in his eyes.

I finally call it a night when all three of my friends have had one too many. Carrie has had way too many and can barely walk at this point.

Bull shows up as if on cue and helps me get my friends to my car. It's a struggle, and I'm sure I should be embarrassed by how loud and rowdy they are being. The irony hits me that of the whole night, we're the ones that have caused the ruckus at the bar, not any of the bikers.

Once they're all in my car, I thank Bull for helping me again. But he doesn't say anything; he just pulls me in for another kiss that has me melting against him. His hands slide up my waist and he teases my nipple through my clothes. I gasp, but all that does is give him more access, and he deepens the kiss and his finger rolls against my hard peak.

If I had a lucid thought I'd pull away. I know I should be offended, but I can't, and I don't. If anything, I push my breast into his hand, and he squeezes me. My head falls back with a loud groan.

He's smiling at me. He knows exactly what he's doing to me. "Call me, Kate." The demand makes him seem mature beyond his years.

When I get into my car, luckily all three of my friends seem to be passed out and missed out on my little display with Bull. I take them all to their houses and by the time I get home, it's late. Walking into the house, I know I should be tired. But my body is still vibrating with desire for Bulldog. I don't think I've ever wanted anyone so much.

I pick up my phone and look at the name he put into it. Bull. I have his number right here. I know there's nothing that can come of this. I know it would only be one night. Darn, I've never done a one-night stand before. Heck, I haven't dated or even seen anyone else naked except for my ex-husband. I put the phone down on the counter. *I can't do this.*

I walk away, but I only get three steps before I'm turning around and running back to the counter. I pick up the phone and start to pace. It's a one-night fling. A single time I can look back on and know that I had some fun and kicked up my heels. I can let myself go and have some fun one night. It's not going to hurt anyone.

I'm not as into texting as his generation, but I figure it's appropriate to see if he's still awake.

Hey, I text him.

Shoot, and then I text him again, *This is Kate. From the bar. Tonight.*

I hit send and then put my hand to my head. Smooth, Kate. Real smooth.

His response is immediate. *I want to see you.*

I don't even know how to flirt or be coy. *Can I come to you?*

Almost immediately I get a text with an address. And then another one that just says *Hurry*.

I fast walk to my bedroom and decide to shower before I leave. I put on my sexiest bra and panties since I figure it'll be the best I can do to compete with the younger, tighter, more agile bodies he's no doubt used to.

Bulldog

What is taking her so long?

I'm standing on my porch, looking up and down the road, hoping to see her car lights soon. It seems like it's been hours since she texted me, but in reality, it's only been thirty minutes.

I reach down and adjust myself. I'm hard enough to use my dick as a fucking jackhammer.

It's almost like I can still feel her in my arms. The way she melted against me on the dance floor and then again by her car, I'd wanted to fuck her both times right where we stood. The ways she kissed me, savoring every stroke of my tongue and tasting me like she was starving for me, made me so hard I couldn't believe how close I was to losing all control. And that's not me. I never lose control. In the military, I was trained to always keep my cool and to never lose my edge. But all of that went out the fucking window when I laid eyes on her tonight.

It was hard enough waiting on her to contact me. I knew I shouldn't push her. She didn't seem the type to like being pressured. But I'd been all of five minutes away from getting a track on her phone and going to her house before she'd texted me.

Her coming to me will make her more comfortable, so I'm willing to wait because I have no intention of taking what I want and skipping out the next morning. No, I already know I want something more than a one-night stand with Kate. I just hope she sees past my tattoos and hard exterior and gives me a real chance.

5

KATE

I drive to his address, which takes me back over into the rougher area of town near the bar. I park my car and look around nervously. There are no neighbors, and I am out in the middle of nowhere. I almost chicken out and go home until I spot Bull standing on his porch, his arms crossed, staring at me.

I no sooner turn off my car and my headlights than he's at my door, opening it for me and helping me out.

"What took you so fuckin' long?" he asks in a deep, raspy voice that sends a thrill of danger down my spine as he shuts the door, takes the keys from my hand, locks up the car, and arms the alarm.

"I... took a shower."

He gets a smirk on his face like I said something funny and takes me into his house. I look around the place briefly. It's clean. Bare, but clean.

I put my hand on the back of his couch, like it's going to steady me. "I, uh, don't normally do this."

He laughs again, and I watch as he puts my keys in his pocket. "I figured that out already. Do you want something to drink?"

"No. No, thank you," I tell him and my mind starts to go crazy. What was I thinking? He could put anything in my drink and no one knows where I am. No one would even know I'm missing until Sunday night when my daughter comes home.

It's really starting to sink in that I've taken a huge risk coming to his place like I did.

Bulldog

I can see the wheels turning in her head again. That responsible part of her that has kept her being careful is no doubt sounding the alarm when it comes to me, and I know it. I don't want her to think and talk herself out of being with me. I can see she's attracted to me, and it's strong enough she's already broken all her safety rules by coming to my house by herself in the first place.

That's good because the way I'm feeling like I'm going to burst at the seams if I don't bury my cock in her any second is going against my own rules. Going after a woman that I see as more than just a piece of ass has always been a red flag. It's how a man gets himself tied down and lets his guard down.

But I know that Kate is different. She's not just different, she's the one I want to let in past the walls. I can't explain it, I can't even begin to try, but I know it's the truth.

I grip her hand and thread our fingers together. I hold them up, looking at them. Mine are hard and callused and hers are soft and feminine, but they fit together perfectly. Just like I know the rest of us will.

"You showered before you came over, why?" I ask, wanting to watch her squirm just a moment longer.

She stammers, saying something about preferring to be clean as I smile down at her. She tries to back away from me, but I just follow her, smiling. When the back of her legs bump into the table, I reach down and take two handfuls of her skirt and pull it up slowly until it's around her waist.

I slide my hand down the front of her body and cup her panty-clad pussy. She's already wet. "Are you trying to hide how wet you are for me?"

I massage my fingers against her, and she's gasping, unable to even answer me. I kiss her lips and her neck, loving the way her breasts are peaked and pressing against my chest.

I kiss down her neck and have to will myself to stop there. I pull away to look at her. Her eyes are closed, lips swollen, and only when I've been staring down at her a few seconds does she finally open her eyes.

"What? Why'd you stop?" she asks, still dazed.

When I pick her up, her arms and legs go around me, and I hold on to her ass and hips to keep her up against me. I stride down the hallway and to the bedroom. I want to throw her onto the bed and dive between her legs, but I don't. Instead I take a seat on the bed and hold her, still straddling me. My dick is painfully stretched against the material of my jeans, but I don't try to adjust. It's like I don't want to make the wrong move here. "I stopped because I know you're a little worried about being here, not knowing me. I saw you second guessing yourself and I don't want that to be between us. So call or send a text to whoever you want to, let them know where you're at." I take a deep breath, taking in the small turn of her nose and the freckles on her face that she tried to hide with makeup but I can still see. I bring my hands up her back and rest on her neck, forcing her to look at me. "Because I want you, Kate. You can leave if that's what you want to do, but don't think I'm letting you go. I won't stop until I have you. Until I've buried my dick so deep inside you there's no way you're going to forget who I am."

She's stubborn, and she lifts her chin at me, almost defiantly. I try to stop the smirk on my face, and I hide it, barely. Without even blinking, she says, "I'm here because I want to be. I'm here because I want to have a good time. It's one night and then I go back to my world. There won't be anything more between us than whatever happens here tonight."

The glint in her eyes tells me that she believes what she's saying. So she's giving me one night. That's it. That's all she wants from me. Fine. Challenge accepted. Now I only need to prove her wrong, because after one taste, I know this is going to be more.

6

KATE

He looks like he may argue with me, but he doesn't. Instead, he lifts me off his lap, and I panic for a minute. Is he pushing me out the door? That's the exact opposite of what I want. I mean, I just told him I wanted a one-night stand. Isn't that what most men would dream of hearing?

I start to turn, but he stops me. "Take your clothes off for me."

I cross my arms on my chest. "You sure are bossy."

He shrugs his shoulders. "It's the army in me."

"You were in the army? I should have guessed that." He does have that air about him. He's disciplined and in control.

"Yes, now take your clothes off."

He's sitting on the edge of the bed, and I reach for the light switch, but he stands up to stop me. "No, lights on. Like you said, if it's one night, I want it all. I want to touch and taste every crevice of your body and I need the lights to do that."

I shiver at his words. I already know what he can do with that tongue and the thought of it on me has me literally shaking as I stand here and take in his words. I could walk out of here. That's what I should do, and a part of me wants to. I know I look different than the women he is usually with. I saw the woman at the bar earlier rubbing his arm and practically begging for him. But I don't move. The fire in his eyes is like a dare to me and the way my body trembles and aches with just him looking at me reminds me that I'm not going anywhere. I want this. I need this.

My skirt is still bunched around my hips, and I unzip it, kicking off my shoes and then sliding the material down my legs. I don't look at him, because if he's disappointed I don't want to see it. I look at a nail on the wall and focus on it. I finish undressing, pulling my shirt over my head and then letting my hands fall to my sides, thankful that I put on the prettiest bra and panties I have.

He's so quiet and doesn't say a word. He moves, taking a step toward me, and my body jerks a little like he's an electric force pulling me in. But still I don't look at him. I can't.

His hands come out, and his finger touches one of my hard nipples. I bite my lip, but I still don't look at him.

His other hand slides down my shoulder and arm, and then he grabs on to my hand. He pulls me toward him and places my hand over the huge bulge in the front of his pants. As soon as I touch him, he groans, and my eyes snap to his.

He smiles, but almost painfully. "That got your attention. Why won't you look at me? Wishing I was someone else?"

I search his eyes and see the muscles in his cheek flex. Is he for real?

I shake my head and then ask him the same. "No. You wishing I was someone else?"

He then shakes his head. "No. I haven't thought of another woman since you walked into the Ride or Die. You're the one I want."

Instinctively, I move closer to him and grip his hard package more firmly in my hand. "I'll give you that. You're a smooth talker."

He shakes his head. "I don't want to talk anymore. I want to taste you."

"And I want to see you now," I tell him, releasing him and tugging at his shirt. He doesn't stop me. I pull it up and he holds his arms up to let me pull it over his head. His chest is hard and the muscles ripple as he moves to help me get the shirt off. I barely drop the shirt to the floor and my hands are on his body, exploring him. He lets me, but not as much as I want.

He stops my hands and holds them against his chest. "It's been a while, and if you want me to last any time at all, you're going to have to quit touching me."

I roll my eyes. "You don't have to lie to me. I'm here already."

He reaches behind me and undoes my bra. "I won't lie to you. Even to get what I want."

He pulls the straps off my shoulders and down my arms before tossing it to the chair on the other side of the room. I want to cover myself, or at least cup my breasts and lift them up. I don't have the same breasts I did in my twenties. Gravity has hit and I'm not too comfortable standing here in front of his perfect specimen of a body with my what could be considered droopy boobs.

As soon as I start to raise my hands, he stops me, grabbing on to each one. "Is this how we're going to do this? You going to try and hide each part of your body I uncover?"

I could lie to him, but I don't. "Probably," I tell him honestly.

He releases one of my hands and cups my breast, flicking his thumb across the hard peak. "No more hiding, Kate, 'cause I want to see it all."

He's being honest. I can tell by the way his eyes have darkened that he wants me. Regardless what I think I look like, he's looking at me like a cake that he can't wait to devour.

I let my body soften at his words and finally nod my head, giving in to him.

He pulls his pants and underwear down in one swoop and I look down at his length as it springs between us. He's large and throbbing for me. But before I can reach for him, he has his fingers in the side of my panties and he's sliding them down my hips. I step out of them and he lays me back on the bed.

He stares down at me for the longest time. He's stroking his cock and pre cum leaks out of the tip and falls down to my belly like a hot spark. I reach down and find it, rubbing it into my skin. He smiles then, a big smile that takes up his face. My whole body is vibrating, wondering where he's going to touch me first. When he bends over and touches his lips to mine, I lift my legs around his waist and hold on to him. His tongue plunges into my mouth, and he mimics the movement with his hips. He slides down my body, kissing along the way, doing exactly what he said he was going to do, tasting every inch of me until he has his head planted between my legs and he's breathing me in.

My legs squeeze around his neck, all my insecurities rearing their ugly head again. That is, until he touches me. When his tongue strokes along my hot, swollen slit, my legs fall apart and I lose all sense of reality. He tunnels his tongue in and out of me, tasting me, devouring me, savoring me by the sounds of it. His hand comes up between us, and when he's circling my bundle of nerves with his finger, I about come off the bed at the sensation.

He's bringing every want, every need I've ever had to

the surface, and he's satisfying me in a way that has never happened before. I don't have to tell him to the left or the right, it's like he knows exactly where and how I need to be touched. When I feel it, my legs raise up, my feet curl, and there's a tug in my lower belly. Already, I'm about to come. I try to back away because I know if already he's eliciting all these feelings in me, I'm not ready for what else he can do. I try to back away, but his arm comes down on my hips, and he raises his head. His chin is dripping with my juices and his eyes are glazed over. "Honey, if you want me to stop, tell me. But I'm begging you to let me finish. Fuck, you taste so good." And when he licks his lips, it does it. My body reacts and I barely scream out, "yes" before he's diving between my legs, and I'm coming on his face.

Bulldog

Her body spasms around me, and I'm climbing up between her legs, ready to drive my cock deep inside her. I reach for the condom on the side table, thankful that I stopped and bought them on my way home tonight. Fuck, I'd take her without one, but I know she wouldn't want that, not yet. But soon.

I slide the rubber over myself and position myself back between her legs. She's looking at me like she's high, and my chest bows a little knowing that I did that to her. I bring my hand to the side of her face, cupping her jaw. "You with me?"

She smiles and nods her head.

"I can't wait any longer, Kate. I have to get inside you."

Her smile deepens, and she opens her legs to me in assurance.

I line myself up and pause before I sink into her. I'm already filling the rubber with precum and I want to be inside her more than anything I've ever wanted in my life. But I'm holding myself back for pure self-preservation. Every wall that I put up is about to be taken down. Whether she realizes it or not, she's about to destroy any resolve I have of keeping my distance. Once I'm inside her, there won't be any coming back from that. I know it. Deep in my chest, I feel it.

So I take a deep breath, hold on to her hips, and plunge deep inside her as her pussy grips on to me and in a sense, makes me hers.

Once I'm seated, her eyes snap open, and she's fully alert now. She's looking up at me and I can tell by the look on her face she feels it too. This isn't two people having fun for the night. This isn't a one-night stand. This is more, way more than either one of us can fully comprehend right now. So I move. I pull almost all the way out and then plunge into her again.

Her hands come up, touching my shoulders, my arms, across my back, until finally, I grab on to them and hold them over her head on the mattress. She lies there, lifting her hips up to meet me at every thrust, and I can't take my eyes off her. She's the most beautiful woman I've ever met, and right now, I'm making her mine. There will never be another man in her life, and there will never be another woman in mine. This is it.

My face is tense and my whole body is pulled tight. She tilts her head to the side. "Come, Bull. I want to feel you throb inside me," she says.

And then I do. I come, pounding into her until I'm fully spent, and I fall down on top of her.

We lie there, breathless for so long I wonder if my heart is ever going to return to its normal pattern. I pull the condom off, tying the end and dropping it in the waste basket next to the bed. I then pull her to me and hold her there. She's the first to speak. "So I guess I should go."

And now, my heart doesn't just slow down. It damn well stops. I already have my arms and legs around her, but I pull her closer into my embrace. "No, you're staying."

She lifts her head from my shoulder and looks up at me. "I'm staying, huh?" And I can tell she's fighting with herself to be indignant that I'm telling her what to do and then also wanting to listen to what I say.

"Oh, yeah, you're staying. I'm not done with you," I tell her and refrain from telling her I never will be.

She does look indignant then. "Done with me?" She smiles and grinds her pussy into my leg that is between hers. "What else do you have planned?"

I pull her on top of me until she's straddling my hips. "Baby, I'm just getting started."

I can tell she's surprised when she feels my cock, already hard again, pressing against her ass, but I pull her down to me, wanting her lips on mine before I take her again... and then again.

7

KATE

He didn't seem to have a problem with my body. He even made me feel sexy, so sexy that I risk going to the kitchen to get a glass of water in only his T-shirt since it's all I can find without making too much noise and waking him up the next day. I would say morning, but looking at my watch, I see that it's already past noon.

I know I should get out of here. My one-night rule seems to have been put to the side because every time I mentioned leaving, he would take my mind off it by another round of sex. How in the world he did what he did last night is beyond me, but I enjoyed every second of it.

I bring the glass to my lips, planning to take a sip, but instead I chug it. I look around the kitchen and am surprised to see that it isn't a bachelor pigsty full of dirty dishes and junk food.

I bring another full glass of water to my lips and can't help but wonder if he drank something or maybe was on something last night. Will he regret sex with me in the sobering light of the day?

I sip at this glass and freeze when I hear him come into the kitchen behind me.

"You look good in my shirt," he says as his arms come around me and his lips nibble on my ear. His hands come up to cup my breasts and I see the tattoos on his knuckles. LOVE HARD.

When I don't say anything, he nuzzles my neck with the stubble of his beard. His cock, hard once again, is pressed into my backside.

Truly confused, I ask him. "I thought I wore you out last night. How can you be hard again?"

"Am I hard?" he asks me, pushing my shoulder down, bending me over, and slipping into me from behind. "Am I?"

And just like that, he's stolen my breath and any question about him wanting me in the full light of day.

It was round three last night that we had the talk and agreed we were both safe to go without a condom, and I'm glad we did. I try not let it weigh too heavily on me how much trust I'm putting into him, but I forget any doubts as he moves in and out of me.

I moan as he fills me up, and it's like he takes great pleasure in those sounds because when I make them, he does whatever he's doing again, but harder... and deeper.

Bulldog

Fuck, I could take this woman back to bed and stay inside her forever. She's moaning and already I'm about to come. She does that to me. Fuck, I could come just looking at her.

"You're so tight, Kate. Fuck, you feel so good. I could stay like this all day, touching you, just like this."

She moans, and her cunt gets hotter and wetter for me. "You like that, don't you? You like it when I talk dirty to you."

Her body trembles, and she starts moving back and forth, pushing her ass against me.

"Fuck yeah, you do. You like my cock inside you. You know you can control me, don't you? You could make me do anything right now, Kate. This pussy is my master," I tell her as I reach around and apply pressure to her clit. She comes undone then, bucking at me until I'm coming and filling her up.

8

KATE

Bulldog calling me out on how hot I get for him has me sort of panicking when the afterglow wears off. I get up when he goes in search of pants, and I start making scrambled eggs. He comes in and takes over and also makes some pancakes.

"Your house is very neat and isn't what I was expecting," I tell him, trying to fill the silence, wondering if I should be going now. And before I can stop myself, I utter the words and even I can hear the jealousy in them. "You must bring a lot of women back to your place and LOVE them Hard like your tattoo says. But I'm not going to forget you. You were incredible."

He sets the plate down in front of me. "I rarely allow women to come to my house and the few times I have I've never fed them."

"Why not?" I can't stop myself from asking.

He shrugs his shoulders. "I don't want them to think they can come back without an invitation."

I blush and smile at him. "Well, I feel special then. I wish I could come back and keep having mind-blowing sex with you. That would be the life." I take a bite of the perfect pancake and moan around the taste on my lips. I know I'm hungry, but the pancake he made is probably the best thing I've had in a while.

But Bulldog invades my thoughts. "Why can't you?"

Bulldog

She looks as if she is either stunned or didn't hear what I said. "Why can't you come back?"

If she's married or has a boyfriend, she won't for long. I don't know where her head's at, but last night just doesn't happen. We were good together. Too good to just chalk it up to a one-night stand.

She shrugs her shoulders. "I've got a boring, secure life that I worked my ass off for, I'm not a partier or a biker girl. Hell, I'm not even a girl. I'm a woman who's old enough to be your mother if I'd started having babies at sixteen."

The age thing again. Fuck that!

I reach across the table and grab on to her hand. "I've lived more than you have in my twenty-four years. While you're sitting here getting all hung up on numbers why don't you consider that I've fought in wars overseas and here at home? I've lost more friends to war than most people dare to even make. I know how short life can be and I know myself well enough to trust my instincts. Right now, they're telling me that you and I aren't finished yet. I want more and I always go after what I want. Life is too short for anything less."

Somewhere in that speech her hand turned in mine and she's holding me now. Her face is red and I'm hoping that my sermon hit home with her. She can say whatever, but it doesn't matter how old she is or how old I am. This, whatever this is happening between us, is good.

She shakes her head. "You're right. You've truly lived while I've been playing it safe. It makes sense when you say it." And she stops there, but I can tell she has more to say. It's plain on her face that the real world, at least hers, won't accept us. That's why I need to show her mine.

I spend the rest of breakfast talking to her and getting to know her. We talk about work, our likes and dislikes, and it's surprising how easy it is to talk to her when our lives are so different.

It's Saturday, and I have no intention of letting her slip away before I finish making the lasting impression that I intend to make on her. I need to show her what my world is like so she'll see how it isn't all she thinks it is, or maybe that it'll be all she thinks it is and more, but as long as I can show her that she'll fit in just fine by my side, we might have a chance of something lasting.

"Let's go out for a ride. And then maybe to the club to meet some of my friends."

As soon as I say the words, I can tell she's searching for a way to say no. "Look, if you don't want to, that's fine. But I promise you'll have fun. And I promise you'll love my friends."

It takes some urging, but finally she agrees. I go out to her car and grab a bag she left in there last night and leave her to shower and get ready while I do the same in the other bathroom. I would give anything to just join her, but I can tell that she needs her space right now, and I need to prove to her that this is more than just sex.

When she comes out in jeans and a T-shirt, I walk up to her and turn her around, instantly cupping her shapely ass. "Be warned. I'm not going to be able to keep my hands to myself tonight."

She just smiles, leaning into my caress. I tug on her hand, pulling her to the door before I change my mind and decide to just keep her here, chained to my bed for the rest of eternity.

She stops in front of my bike and looks at it skeptically. "I'm not getting on that. I like to live."

Her little nose is turned up at the idea of getting on my bike, and I would make fun of her, but this is too important. "C'mon. You trust me, don't you?"

She wants to say no, anything to stop her from getting on the back of the bike, but she doesn't. "Yes," she mutters.

"Good." I sit down on the bike and scoot forward, raising it upright. I hold my hand out to her, hoping she doesn't turn me down. "One ride. If you don't like it, we'll come back and get my truck."

Finally she agrees and gets onto the back. As soon as she sits down, I grab on to her thighs and pull her into me, until I can feel every inch of her pressed against my back.

"Ah, I see why you wanted to ride the bike," she jokes, sliding her hand down my chest and letting it settle low on my belly, her knuckles grazing against my crotch.

I cup her hand, holding her against me. "You keep this up, we won't be going anywhere but back to my bedroom."

She laughs and pulls her hand away. "No way, mister. You promised me a ride, so you're giving me one."

She was worried a second ago and now she seems to be looking forward to it. So before she can change her mind, I start the bike, pull out of the driveway, and head straight to Hollow Oak Hill.

It takes twenty minutes to get there, but only because I'm taking it slow. When I stop, with the view of Hollow Lake in front of us, you can't help but take in the beauty of it all. There's a sigh at my back and I ask her, "It's beautiful, isn't it?"

She nods her head, but still doesn't say a thing.

"You want to get off and stretch your legs or ride some more?"

I hold my breath, waiting for her answer. Her thighs tighten around me. "I think I'd like to ride some more."

I squeeze her hand at my chest before taking off again. We ride all the back roads and down into town before circling back and ending up at the Ride or Die.

When she gets off, her legs start to buckle, and she would fall to the ground if I wasn't there to hold on to her. As soon as I have her upright, she's looking up at the sign for the bar. "This isn't a good idea. I mean, look at me. My hair's a mess, I'm a mess..."

She's running her fingers through her ponytail, trying to show me what a mess she is, but in my eyes, she's perfection.

"You're perfect," I tell her, holding her to me. I've discovered that if I have her in my arms, she's more likely to do what I ask. "Come in with me."

She takes a deep breath and pulls back her shoulders. "Fine, let's go."

I have no qualms on how my brothers will react to Kate. I hold her hand and keep her near me, wanting her to know that no matter what, she's safe with me.

Luckily, Roxy and Gage are here tonight, and they hang out with us. I turn down the beer that Peaches, the new bartender, is offering me and go with water instead. I'm driving around precious cargo and I know I need to keep a clear head.

Kate is a bundle of nerves, but Roxy makes her feel right at home. They spend a lot of time talking, and although I can't hear them, it must be something good by the way Kate is smiling at me. Even when I pull her to my lap, she doesn't resist. She just melts into me with one arm around my back and the other on my chest.

Roxy is complaining about the music. Conley, the club president, loves his seventies rock. Roxy goes to the jukebox and comes back as a new popular dance song comes on. "Conley isn't happy that I'm trying to update his music selection, but he did compromise and lets me play a few current hits a night. Let's dance, Kate."

Roxy doesn't even give Kate a chance to refuse. She pulls her from my lap and I barely get a kiss before she's on the dance floor. I don't take my eyes off her.

She's having fun and I'm so glad that I brought her here. It's nice to see her let loose.

"Earth to Bulldog. Come in." I shake my head as Gage waves his hand in front of my face.

"Sorry," I mutter, still watching Kate.

"You can take your eyes off her. Everyone saw you come in with her, and no one is going to mess with her," Gage says.

I take my eyes off Kate and look over at Gage. I can't help but smirk. "Really? Is that why you can't take your eyes off Roxy, Mr. Vice President?"

He laughs and shrugs his shoulders. "She's a lot better than looking at your ugly mug."

I don't disagree with him. Instead I get down to business. "How's it going? Anything I need to know?"

There's a vein throbbing in his forehead, so I know there's something going on, even though he's trying to act like he's just having a night out with his wife and the mother of his child. "Yeah. No matter how much we try to stay clean, our past keeps catching up with us. The Blue Devils are encroaching on our territory. We've spotted them in town a few times, and although they haven't tried anything, I know something's coming. I can feel it in my gut."

I know exactly what he's talking about. I've learned to trust my gut over the years and it's never steered me wrong. "I'll keep an eye out. Let me know if I need to do anything."

We sit there and talk about the happenings in the club before a slow song comes on. I get up and walk out to the dance floor and open my arms, and Kate instantly steps into them. Gage does the same with Roxy. I never thought I'd see the day when our gruff vice would be on the dance floor, but I've learned that women can do some amazing things to a man in love.

Kate running her hands up my chest brings me back to the present. She looks so happy, so at ease, and I wish I could keep her like this always. She doesn't have to tell me that our worlds are different. I know they are. My world accepts us, no questions asked. The men of the Heartlands would defend her to the death if I asked them to. But her world? I have a feeling it's not going to be the same. She can try to shy away from this all she wants, but it's happening. We're happening.

9

KATE

I stretch in my bed and snuggle into Bull's heat. He's right; last night was perfect. We had a good time. If his friends had any qualms about my age, they sure didn't show it. They all went out of their way to make me feel welcome. Gage, Roxy, Ranger, Jaxon, Beckham, all the names started running together. They were a wild bunch, but it's obvious they care about each other like family.

We had a great time, playing pool, dancing, and hanging out with his friends. And when it was time to leave, I asked him if he wanted to come to my house, mostly because I didn't want it to end. The one-night stand has turned into so much more, and even though I knew it couldn't last, I could at least enjoy it through the weekend.

So he took me to his house, I picked up my car, and he followed me home on his bike. I look over at him in my bed, surrounded by the white walls and furniture, with the white sheet pulled halfway up his body. He looks good in my bed, I can't help but think.

But instead of dwelling on that, I go to the kitchen and start on breakfast. I'm only out of bed a few minutes before he's at my back, his body surrounding mine, and he's breathing me in. "I missed you," he says before he kisses my neck.

I can't help but stiffen at his words. This is good, almost too good. But it can't last.

I turn in his arms, and when I do, I look out the window into the driveway and notice my ex-husband's car pulling up. Shoot.

Luckily, I'm dressed in shorts and a T-shirt, and I tell Bull to stay put.

He looks surprised, but luckily doesn't follow me as I step out the door and close it behind me. If I had to guess, he's spotted my fourteen-year-old daughter out the window and is probably a little stunned. I never did mention to him that I have a daughter.

I walk on to the porch and wait for Charlie and Emma to come up the steps. Before I can even hug or say hello to Emma, Charlie is on me. "Whose bike is that?"

I pull Emma in for a hug. And barely refrain from answering Charlie with a "it's none of your business," but hopefully the look on my face tells him exactly what my thoughts are.

I ask Emma instead, "What are you doing home so early? I thought you were staying until later tonight."

She rolls her eyes, like only a teenage girl can. "Chloe wanted to go to the mall with me and my friends. I refused to hang out with her and so I had Dad bring me home."

I should tell her that she needs to respect adults, but Chloe is the one that Charlie cheated on me with, and I know Emma blames her for the breakup. Regardless, I'm not going to get into all that now.

"Whose bike is that, Kate?"

Finally, I do answer him. This is my house and I don't owe him anything. "A friend of mine is inside. But really, it's none of your business."

"None of my business? I bought this house." He starts to yell at me.

I hold my hand up to stop him. "Go inside, Emma. I'll be there in a minute."

She looks between us and walks inside, and I turn back to Charlie, the man that still seems to think he can control what I do.

Bulldog

Luckily, I went in and put on clothes before sitting back down at the dining room table. I can no longer see the man and young girl outside, but I can hear the man. The door opens and in walks the daughter, a younger image of Kate.

She looks taken back. "Who are you?"

"Uh, I'm a friend of your mother's. I'm Bull."

She nods her head. "I'm, uh, Emma." She sits down on the couch and with the open concept, she's just a few feet away from me. It's awkward for me, and I know it is for her.

The voices get louder outside, and I ask Emma, "Does he always talk to her like that?"

Emma's face scrunches up. "Yep, always. She always wanted me to have my mother and father in the picture and I think she thought I wanted her to put up with that mess. Thankfully, he cheated on her and that was the last straw."

I can't help but wonder how old she is. She seems pretty wise for a kid.

When the voices get even louder, I've had enough. "I'll be right back," I tell Emma and walk out the door, shutting it firmly behind me.

The man is staring at me incredulously, but I ignore him. I pull Kate against me. "Go inside."

She turns in my arms with fire in her eyes, but I smile down at her. "Go inside, please?"

She snaps her mouth closed and finally nods her head. Without another look at the other man on the porch, she walks inside. When the door shuts, I turn back to him with a menacing look on my face. "Hey, Judge Hawthorne."

"How do you know me? I don't know you."

I just laugh. "I'm Bulldog. I'm with the Heartlands MC and you're on our payroll."

He looks confused. “Payroll? I’m not on your payroll. What are you talking about?”

I shake my head and laugh again. “You’re right, not anymore. Not since we went on the straight and arrow. But before, when we did all the drug runs, the guns, all of it, you were right there with us. You were in our back pocket. We have more than enough evidence to take you down.”

He looks alarmed for a minute and then shakes his head. “No way. If you try to take me down, you’re going down with me.”

“We’re smarter than you give us credit for, Judge. We have everything tied to you. Nothing has our name on it.”

He sneers, showing me the man I know he is. “What do you want?”

“You’ll never talk to Kate like that again. And if I hear of you mistreating her or your daughter again, I’ll end you. And don’t even test me. You know I can do it.”

I expect him to argue. I expect something, but he really is a cowardly piece of shit by the way he just nods his head and walks away from me, down the steps, and to his car.

As soon as he pulls out, Kate comes out the door. "I don't need a keeper. I can take care of myself..."

But I stop her and pull her into my arms, breathing her in. "I know. But if you think I'll stand by and let anyone mistreat you and talk to you like that, you're mistaken. That's over."

She wants to argue. I think she likes to argue with me, maybe because she likes the making up part too. I don't know, but I'll stand firm on this. I keep hold of her until she's softening in my arms. We stand there for I don't know how long, until I finally ask her, "So you have a daughter huh?"

She looks up into my face and I can see the guilt she has for not telling me. "Yep, she's fourteen going on thirty."

I nod my head in acceptance. I don't know what she thought, but a kid is not going to run me off. At this point, nothing will.

I start to tell her that, but the door opens. Kate freezes in my arms and I know she wants to pull away, but I stop her. Emma looks between us and smiles. "It looks like you were starting breakfast when I got here so I finished it up. It will be ready in a minute." She turns and goes inside.

Kate looks up at me. “So I guess you’ll stay for breakfast.”

I kiss her lips before pulling back. “I wouldn’t miss it.”

I don’t know what I expected, but sitting down with Emma and Kate is a whole new experience for me. They laugh and have a good time, making jokes. One of them being Emma’s cooking.

Emma laughs at her mother’s joke. “I’m sorry. I’m still working on the eggs.”

I jump in and take a bite, swallowing down the overdone egg. “I like mine done.”

And that wins her over. “See, Bull knows what he’s talking about.”

Kate sits back in her chair. “Okay, I know when I’m being ganged up on. Fine, the eggs are good.”

And as we all laugh, Emma asks, “So are you two seeing each other?”

Kate chokes on her food, and I reach for her, patting her on the back. When she’s finally able to breathe again, Emma holds her hands up. “I was just asking. But I like him, Mom. I think he’s good for you.” She gets up from her chair and sets her plate in the sink. "And since I cooked, I'll leave the dishes for you all."

We both watch her leave, and I wait for Kate to smile at me, to feel better knowing her daughter is okay with us, but it doesn't happen. She does smile at me, but it doesn't quite reach her eyes.

I grab on to her hand and she looks almost sad as she looks at our intertwined fingers. She's already trying to give up on us, but I'm not going to let her.

10

KATE

I wake up to my alarm that I had set for six am on Monday morning so I can get ready for work. I go through my routine, drop Emma off at school, and go to work. I can't help but think that being with Bull was like a dream now that I'm back in the real world.

My friends stop by my office and ask me if I ever called the hottie from Friday night, and I'm surprised by how quickly I lie and say I didn't.

The morning flies by and I've lost count of the number of times I've thought of Bull. I've already accepted the fact that I'm going to break my own rule and call him as soon as I'm alone in my car on my lunch break. My friends would die of jealousy if they knew just how incredible my weekend truly was.

Lunch hour has finally arrived, and I stand up to get

my things together so I can leave for lunch. I'm in a hurry, so I bend over my desk to grab my purse from the bottom desk drawer.

When two strong hands squeeze my butt, I let out a surprised squeal and straighten up, ready to punch whichever perv from tech decided it was okay to touch me.

But it's not a perv from tech. No, right now, it's worse. It's Bull.

The door to my office is open and a crowd has started to gather. Many of them look concerned and I think I hear one of them ask if they should call security.

I can feel my face burning and I wave them off. "No, everything is fine. He's uh, here to see me."

He crowds into me, dipping his head. "You look so hot in that skirt. It makes me want to yank it up and – "

I look at the crowd out in the hall and back to Bull. "Whoa-kay there, that's plenty. Thank you for the... uh, compliment. Is there something wrong? Something you needed?"

He reaches for my hand, but I pull it back.

"Uh, I came to take you to lunch."

I try to look him in the eye, but I can't lie to him, looking into his trusting eyes. "I shouldn't leave for lunch because I have so much work to do." I point to the stacks of work still in my inbox, hoping he'll accept my answer and leave.

Bulldog

I take in her deep blush and look over at the nosy crowd watching and know why she's acting like she is. With barely a nod, I walk away from her, and I'm pretty sure I pass her friends from the other night. They are all gawking at me. But I just look straight ahead and try to hide how pissed I am right now.

Kate follows me but doesn't say a word until we're out of the building. As soon as the door shuts behind her, she speeds up. "Bull, wait."

I turn on her and she stops in her tracks. I know I shouldn't, not here, not with how mad I am, but I call her out on her behavior. "You're embarrassed of me and worried about what other people might think. I can't waste my life living like that. I'm proud to be with someone that makes me feel the way you do, but if that's not enough for you, then fuck it."

She's saying my name over and over, but I don't stop. I get on my bike and pull out of the parking lot. The whole way I'm swearing to myself that I'm not going to have anything to do with her again.

Kate

I return to my office and it seems everyone is staring at me. My boss brings me to his office to reprimand me on proper office etiquette.

My friends, who'd been encouraging me before, are scandalized now by my choice to actually call him.

I finish out the workday and am miserable when I get home. It was bad having everyone look at me like I'd done something wrong. It was bad when my boss threatened to write me up for allowing a visitor to grope me openly in front of so many people.

But the worst part was when Bulldog looked at me like I'd betrayed him. It was worse to hear the truth of my feelings come out of his mouth in that cold, pained tone of his voice. Worst of all was watching him leave and knowing that I deserved to be left behind.

I try to hide my sadness from Emma, but she notices it because she asks me when Bulldog will be around again.

With sadness, I tell her what I did today and that he probably won't ever be around again.

"He'll come around. Besides, Mom, aren't you always telling me you shouldn't care what other people think? You should practice what you preach." She opens the refrigerator and peers in. "Can we order Chinese?"

I nod and she goes about ordering the food, but I'm still stuck on what she said. I really should practice what I preach. Man, did I screw up.

I put on my pajamas, the soft ones that are almost threadbare, but they always bring me comfort, and then I sit on the couch with a glass of wine.

The knock at the door sounds and I grab my wallet and open it, pulling my cash out. When I raise my head, I look straight into the eyes of Bull. He shakes the wetness from his hair. "I couldn't stay away," he admits, his hair wet from the rain and his clothes clinging to his hot body.

I'm so happy to see him I throw my arms around him and pull him into the house.

11

BULLDOG

I'm glad that I second-guessed myself. I swore I was going to walk away, but only a few hours later, I've already convinced myself to go see her.

She's holding me, and I know I'm getting her wet. I definitely wasn't thinking because I drove over here on my bike with dark clouds in the sky. I knew it was going to rain, but I didn't care.

She pulls from my arms and is no sooner gone than she's coming back to me, holding out a towel. She wraps it around me, but I reach for her again, wanting her in my arms.

She puts her chin on my chest and looks up at me. "I'm so sorry for how I acted, but you have to know that I'm not embarrassed of you. All of that was about me."

I loosen my hold on her because even though I've never been the brunt of the "it's not you, it's me" breakup, this is how I imagined it would start.

She pulls me over to the dining room chair and starts pulling off my boots. She gets one off and then looks at me. "I'm embarrassed by how old I am and how selfish I am that I want you when you're so young and you have your whole life still ahead of you."

She yanks on the other shoe and when she drops it, I pull her to my lap. I hate that she's so hung up on our difference in age. "I couldn't be more proud to have you on my arm. I didn't last one day trying to stay away from you, and I don't think I can. I know I don't want to."

Something between a laugh and a sob escapes her throat, and she's pulling me in for a kiss. I know we have so much to talk about, but I can't dismiss her. I can't pull away from her.

We kiss and get lost in each other until I hear footsteps coming down the hall and pull away from her. It's completely obvious what we were doing, but other than the pink in her cheeks, Kate doesn't try to hide it.

Emma comes around the corner and I smile at her. "Hey, Emma."

She doesn't even look surprised to see me. But she does roll her eyes. "Thank goodness. I haven't seen Mom so upset, well, I don't think I've ever seen her that upset before."

Kate gets embarrassed and tries to hide her face from me, but I stop her by tipping her chin up to look at me. "I don't want you upset. Ever."

She pulls herself from my arms. "I'm not. Now."

The doorbell rings again and Emma announces, "Chinese."

Kate

I go to the door and swap cash for the bags of food. Bull, Emma, and I sit down, and I spoon out a little bit of everything on everyone's plate.

I watch as Bull and Emma talk, and once she finds out he was in the army, she asks him a gazillion questions. I wait for him to get fed up with all of them, but he doesn't. And I notice that he talks to her like he would anyone else, instead of like he's talking to a child, which seems to go a long way with Emma.

"So, how'd you go from being in the army to being a bouncer at a bar?"

"Emma!" I say, alarmed that she's asked him such a thing.

But he just laughs. "It's a legitimate question. It's okay."

But still, I tell him, "You don't have to answer that."

"No, I can. It's fine. I saw so much when I was in the army. I lost a lot of good friends, my fiancée left me while I was over there..."

Emma and I both gasp, and he looks at me apologetically, like he should have already told me that, but I shrug my shoulders. "How could she do that?"

He takes a drink of water and sets the glass down. "It's fine. Some people aren't cut out for a life of waiting. It's good. It all worked out. But when I got out of the army, I had trouble adjusting. That's when Saint and Ranger and the rest of the guys sort of brought me in and made me part of the family. I've been the bouncer since I got home, but I'm trained in defense and security detail."

Emma takes it all in, and I'm proud of the way she listens and asks intelligent questions. She's growing up too fast.

And then she turns to me. "So I graduate soon." And here it is, she wants something.

"Graduate?" Bull asks.

I shake my head, because I can tell he's confused. "She's graduating eighth grade."

"Ooooh!" Emma claps her hands together and bounces in her seat. "You have to come to my graduation."

He doesn't even have to think about it. He nods his head. "Yeah, sure, if it's okay with your mom. I'll be there."

I shake my head at my daughter and then look at Bull. "It's almost two months away. You don't have to commit to going."

He smiles and reaches for my hand. "I'll be there. Just tell me when and where."

Emma goes into the spiel of when and where the graduation is. I notice that Bull takes his phone out and puts the details in his calendar and then sends a text.

"It's all set. I've requested the night off and I have it in my calendar. I'll be there. So what do you want for your graduation?"

Emma starts to speak, looks at me, and then back to Bull. She recites exactly what we've rehearsed. "You don't need to bring a gift. I'll just be happy if you are there."

Bull smirks, because it's obvious that Emma has rehearsed the line. He laughs. "Okay, maybe money then. That way you can get what you want."

"Yes!" Emma pumps her arms, but instead of admonishing her, I let her run off back to her bedroom.

As soon as she's out of earshot, I tell him, "You know you can't make promises that you don't plan to keep. Plus, it's two months away."

He shrugs his shoulders. "I'll be there."

I know I look at him doubtfully, but it doesn't stop him from pulling me into his lap. "So, let's talk."

I can't help it, I tense up. He nuzzles my neck, and the stubble rubs along my jawline. "About what?" I ask him.

I can feel his smile against my chin. "Well, I was thinking that since your daughter's in the other room, and we really can't do anything, I could at least sit here, hold you, and tell you everything I would like to be doing to you."

Then I soften in his arms. This I can handle.

He whispers against my skin, reminding me in words what it was like for him to be inside me and how much he wants to be there again. He goes on and on, telling me everything he feels being with me, beside me, and in me. And well, I thought I could handle it, but I literally melt against him, breathing hard and wanting him more than I've ever wanted anything before in my life.

12

KATE

Two months of being Bulldog's "girlfriend"—because I refuse to call myself his ol' lady—has been exhilarating, fulfilling, and the most fun I've ever had.

Going to work has become more difficult not only because I resent the way I was treated by them about Bull but also because everything has changed in my life. My old life now feels like a lie, and yet I can't let it go.

This should be so much more difficult than it is. Charlie has not questioned me again about Bull, he acts like he doesn't even notice him, but he's been nicer to me and Emma, better than he's ever been.

We've been out with Bull's friends a few times, and they accept us. But most importantly, Emma is over the moon about Bull and me being together. Pretty much when he offered to go to the school and talk to her math teacher after he'd given her a bad grade sealed the deal for her. Bull was convinced it was unfair and that he could get the teacher to raise her grade, but I was able to stop him before he got out the door. I convinced him that Emma needed to learn to stand up for herself, but it meant so much to me—well, Emma and me both—that he was willing to stand up for her.

But even though Emma likes him, I still haven't let him spend the night when she's here, and he respects that. But man, there are some nights I want to say screw it and let him sleep over.

Tonight, Emma's at her dad's and I'm home alone. Bull is at work and I had planned to spend the evening getting caught up on things I've been letting slide. But I don't want to. Right now, what I'd like to do is go to the bar and watch my man at work.

So I spend the next half hour getting ready to go over to the Ride or Die.

Bulldog

It's a wild night at the bar. It's barely ten o'clock and already the bar is full of people. There have already been two fights and one of the women, a regular lately, has already been causing a ruckus. It seems she's had her sights on Saint, and Cat is not handling it well.

I pick up the woman with the thought that I'm going to carry her outside, but she has other ideas. She twists in my arms, wrapping her body around mine, and I struggle to walk to the front door. I move my head to see around her and the first thing I spot is Kate coming in.

She looks at the woman in my arms and then back to me. I'm struggling to put the woman on her feet, but she just slides down my body and forces her lips to mine. I tear myself away from her just in time to see the hurt look on Kate's face before she turns around and runs from the building.

I am no longer worried about the woman. I chase after Kate. "Kate! Kate! Stop," I holler after her.

But she keeps going and doesn't stop until she's standing next to her car. She turns to face me. "It's no big deal, Bull. We weren't serious. You can have whoever you want."

I should be apologizing to her, explaining to her what she saw, but instead, all I see is red. "That's crap and you know it, Kate. We are serious. You're the one I want."

She laughs, literally laughs in my face. "It didn't look like it back there." She shakes her head. "No, you know what? It's good I came. It's good I saw this."

I throw my hands up in the air. "What? Me doing my job? Because that's what you saw. I was removing her from the bar."

She crosses her arms over her chest and the look she's giving me tells me exactly how mad and hurt she is. "Oh, I didn't realize kissing women was part of your job. Good to know."

I start to explain, but Cat comes out the entrance of the bar, dragging the same woman I had in my arms only seconds ago. Cat pulls her by the hair until she's standing up and then punches her. The woman falls to the ground, and Cat stands over top of her. "You don't mess with other women's men, you piece of trash."

She's huffing and puffing, and I know if I don't intervene, Cat's going to do worse and then Saint's going to be all pissed off that I let his woman do my job for me. "I got it, Cat. Just leave her there."

Cat walks over to me, holding her hand with the other. She hit her pretty good and she's probably hurt her hand. She stops in front of Kate. "You must be Kate. Bull's told me all about you. Sorry we had to meet this way, but I think she understands now to keep her hands off men that are taken," Cat says to Kate as she gestures over to the woman that is still lying on the ground.

Kate says hi, and they talk a few minutes and I wonder if everything is okay, but as soon as Cat walks away, Kate's face is closing up again. "Do you see, I wasn't with that woman. She's drunk, nothing was happening."

But Kate isn't looking very forgiving right now. "No. Look, this isn't my thing, Bull. It's good I saw this. I'm too old for this kind of thing."

I stand there stunned. I thought we were done with the age thing. "Age doesn't have anything to do with it. And you know what, neither does what you just saw. You're scared, Kate. Because you know how I feel about you and I know you feel the same for me. But you're scared. You want to keep playing it safe. Hiding me away from your friends, your family. It's like you were waiting on me to screw up. But I didn't. I was doing my job. If you honestly think I could ever want someone else in my arms that isn't you, then we don't have a lot to say to each other."

I know I've gone too far. There's fire flashing in her eyes, and she stubbornly turns away from me and opens her car door. I want to go to her. I want to do whatever I have to do to make this right, but I don't. I can't. I stand here and watch her, hoping she's going to make the right choice.

When she takes a deep breath, my nerves start to settle because I think she may be coming to her senses. But instead, she pummels me. "In the end, me walking away right now is the right thing to do. We aren't meant to be together. The age thing, and everything else. We're just too different. You'll be glad it's over, that I ended it now instead of later."

I want to fight. I want to scream and punch something, but instead I say as calmly as I can muster, "No, I won't be glad that you walked away from me, from us, Kate. You're the only woman I've ever loved, and it sucks that you're giving up on us because of this."

I walk away then, back toward the bar and punch the brick wall. It hurts, but nothing like the pain I'm feeling in my chest.

She stands at her car and watches me for the longest time. I lean against the wall, breathing heavily and watching her get into her car and drive away.

13

KATE

"What's wrong, Mom?" Emma asks me.

I smile at her, the best that I can. I've tried my best to not let her see how upset I've been, but of course she notices. She notices everything.

"Nothing. I'm fine. I'm excited about your graduation tonight. What do you want to do to celebrate afterwards?" I ask her, trying to get her off the subject of me.

She rolls her eyes at me and I'm beginning to figure out that this is definitely a teenage phase that I don't like. "Mom! We're going for pizza afterwards, remember? Me, you and Bull. Where is he anyway?"

I reach out and rub her arm. "He's not coming."

She stares back at me like I've grown a second nose before finally shaking her head. "He'll be there, Mom."

I press my lips together, hating to disappoint her, especially on her big day. But it's better for her to realize it now, instead of later. "No, he won't, honey."

But she just laughs and pats me on the back. "Yes, he will, Mom."

She twirls around in her new dress, all excited that she got a new outfit and even has makeup on today for the occasion.

"You look beautiful, Emma," I tell her honestly, all the while being eaten up with guilt. I'm the reason she's going to be let down tonight. I'm usually smarter than this, but I let my feelings get the best of me and didn't even consider how this was going to affect Emma.

We no sooner get to the school than Emma heads to the backstage of the auditorium and I go to the seat that my parents are saving for me. I see Charlie across the way and his girlfriend Chloe is sitting with him.

"You should have stayed with him," my mother whispers to me when she sees me looking at Charlie.

I turn, stunned. "He cheated on me, Mother. With that woman."

A flicker of irritation shines in her eyes. "So?"

"So? So I'm not staying with someone that cheats on me. That's crazy that you even think I should. I mean, what would I be teaching my daughter by being with someone like that?" I ask, getting louder with each word.

My thoughts stray to Bull. He wouldn't cheat on me. I know he wouldn't. I may have gone a little crazy last night, but I think it was more jealousy and my own insecurities than anything. What was I thinking walking away from him? He's the best man I know.

My dad pats my mom on her shoulder, and we all turn to the stage. We watch the whole graduation, and I couldn't be more proud of Emma when she wins multiple academic and even some athletic awards.

Emma looks at me through the crowd and then I notice her beaming toward the back of the auditorium. I turn slightly in my chair and look to the back of the room. There stands Bull with a bouquet of flowers, smiling ear to ear at Emma.

My heart starts to race. *He came.*

I sit on the edge of my seat through the rest of the ceremony. Afterward, I look for Emma, but when I finally find her she has gone straight to Bull. He hands her flowers and a card.

My mom seems to be racing me to where they stand, and she stops in front of Bull. "What are you doing? You're too old for her."

Emma laughs. "Grandma, he's Mom's boyfriend. He's with her."

I swear my mother's eyebrows raise to her hairline she's so stunned. Emma then decides to go in even more detail. "At least she should be. He's better to us than Dad ever was."

I'm stunned and am too speechless to say anything. I knew that Emma was having trouble with her father, but I had no idea that she realized how little he had to do with us through the years. I thought I had done a good job filling his emptiness.

Bull doesn't even look at me. I know I should introduce him to my mother, but I don't, and after a hug with Emma, he turns to leave.

My parents are looking at me like I've been dating a senior in high school. Judging and thinking the words without even trying to understand.

Suddenly, it's clear. I can finally see that Bull is the only one whose opinion I care about, and it's because I love him. I love Bull.

Taking a page out of his book, I walk toward him. "Fuck it."

I get in front of him to stop him from leaving. Once I get him to stop, I put my hands on his chest. "I'm sorry, Bull. I love you and I know I was crazy..."

But he doesn't let me finish. He pulls me into his arms, his grip tight on my shoulders. "Say it again."

"I'm sorry."

He shakes his head. "Not that."

I look at him with a question in my eyes. "I love you?"

He draws a deep, audible breath. "That's it. That's all I need to hear."

And then he kisses me. In front of Emma, my parents, and I'm sure my ex husband is around somewhere. There's a collective gasp behind me, but I don't care, because this, right here, in Bull's arms, is what I need. I choose him.

Bulldog

Never in a million years is this how I thought this would play out. I was a dick last night to everyone. I went home and fought with myself on going over to her house and trying to convince her that we are right for one another. And now this.

I knew I had to come tonight. There's nothing that would've kept me away. I promised Emma I would be here, and even if it did feel like I was ripping my heart out seeing Kate again and not being able to touch her, I had to do it.

But when Kate grabs me, tells me she loves me, and kisses me—fuck, it's what dreams are made of. I know she's telling me she doesn't care what anyone else thinks anymore with the kiss, making it a million times hotter than any kiss we've shared before. Her smile is gorgeous when I pull back to look at her. There's not even a hint of self-consciousness or doubt.

I rub my fingers on her chin so she looks up at me. With my heart in my eyes, I ask her, "So we're doing this?"

Instead of insecurity, a pink flush comes to her cheeks. "We're definitely doing this."

And I kiss her again. Because I can't resist.

I don't know how long it lasts, but we break apart when Emma comes to stand beside us. "So I told Grandma and Grandpa we were meeting them at the restaurant. Do you want me to ride with them?"

I pull Emma under one arm and put my other around Kate. "No, we're ready. Pizza, right?"

Emma just smiles at the both of us, letting me know that she's happy with Kate and me being together too. "Yep, pizza."

Then I take my girls out to celebrate.

14

KATE

We had a fun night at the pizza place where Bull gave Emma and her friends way too much money that they spent in the gameroom. Charlie and Chloe even showed up and it helped me so much having Bull there with me. Charlie has been a completely different person, and I can't help but wonder if Bull has something to do with it.

It's later and Emma went home with her grandparents, so I'm lying in my bed with Bull. I'm sprawled across him, looking up at him, running my hand across his hard chest. "So there's something we need to talk about."

He looks worried for a minute until I smirk at him, and he knows it's going to be okay. He pushes the hair off my face. "Okay, let's hear it."

“I think if we’re really going to make a go of this –“

He interrupts me. “There’s no question. You said it. You love me. There’s no take backs.”

I chuckle against him and he pulls me further across him, until his hard shaft is positioned between my legs. “Again? How are you hard again?”

He just looks at me full of cockiness. “I’m always ready any time I’m around you.” He tickles my sides and then groans when my leg grazes his cock.

His hands slide down my back to rest on my ass, holding me still and against him. “Really. What is it? What do we need to talk about?”

“Well, I think I need to know your real name.”

He laughs, opens his mouth, and then closes it again. “You promise not to laugh?”

I run my fingers across my chest. “Cross my heart.”

He looks up at the ceiling. “Oliver. My name is Oliver.”

I gasp, never having expected that. I do my best to hold it in, but he can feel my body vibrating against his.

"Is it that funny, Kate? Really? You promised not to laugh."

"I'm not laughing!"

At the look he gives me, I bust out, unable to hold it anymore. He rolls me underneath him and I try to contain my laughter, but I can't. "Oliver? You don't look like an Oliver."

"Har, har. You're funny." But then the smile drops from his face. "Now I need to talk to you about something."

He looks so serious that I start to slide out from underneath him, but he makes me stay put. "Okay." I take a deep breath. "What is it?"

"I can't give up the Heartlands. They're like family to me. I can't just walk away from them."

I push him away and I do sit up then until I'm cross legged in front of him, and I pull the sheet up my body to cover myself. He looks so worried after making that announcement that I grab on to his hand. "I never asked you to leave the Heartlands. I wouldn't do that."

"I know. But I want you to know everything that's going through my head. I am going to quit the bar.

But don't worry, I'll get a job at the garage or the hardware store, something."

I hold his hand between the two of mine. "I don't care where you work, Bull. You should keep your job if that's what you want to do."

"I want you to trust me."

"I do. I apologized for the other night. That was more about me than anything else. I trust you and if that's what you want to do, you should do it. I'm not stopping you," I assure him, wanting him to know that I accept him for who he is.

"I'm glad you said that, but I'm still going to get another job. I want to be able to see you at night. I don't ever want there to be a reason for you to doubt me. I want to be available to you, and I don't want to miss stuff. Working at Ride or Die, I would. So I'm on the hunt for a new job."

I start to argue with him, but I can tell he's already made his mind up. "Fine. Whatever you want to do. But I love you as a bouncer, I love you as Bull, Bulldog, Oliver, whatever. I'm here for it."

He pushes me backwards and lowers himself on top of me. "That's good, baby, because I wasn't giving you an option."

Putting my arms around his neck, I pull him down until my lips touch his, but he pulls back really quick. “I love you, Kate.”

I smile. “I know you do.”

EPILOGUE

BULLDOG

Six Months Later

"What is the matter with you?" I ask Kate for the third time tonight.

She keeps flipping through the channels and mutters, "Nothing."

I don't take my eyes off her, though. I know there's something going on with her. The last six months have been the best of my life. Every possible minute we've spent together.

"Come here," I tell her, pulling her into my lap.

She comes willingly, but her mood doesn't seem to lighten any. Emma is in her room for the night and so it's just us now.

She curls up in my lap, and I try to get her to look at me. "Talk to me. I know something's bothering you."

Her lower lip comes out in a pout. "Are you going to stay the night?"

I shake my head. "You know I don't feel right doing that, not with Emma here. We don't want her to get the wrong idea about how things work."

Normally, she agrees with me, but tonight, she just turns back to the television. Which is a tell anyway because she never watches television. "All right."

I take the remote from her hand and flip it off before tossing it to the chair across from us. I position Kate to where she has to look at me and demand, "Talk to me. Do you want me to leave? Is that what this is about?"

"No!" She leans into me. "I don't want you to leave. I want you to stay. I want to wake up in the morning with you next to me. I'm tired of this and I know, I know, I'm the one that started the rule about no sleepovers when Emma's home, but I mean let's face it. She loves you. She knows we're together. I just don't understand why you don't want to be with me."

"Don't want to be with you?" I take a deep breath and let it out. Our worlds have changed so much in the last six months. I took a job at the hardware store and am already managing the place. Kate was fed up with the uptight way things were happening at her office, and so she started her own accounting firm, which is doing great, and she's been super busy. So much has changed... except how I feel about her. If nothing else, I love her more than I ever dreamed possible. "Do you really think I don't want to be with you?"

She shrugs her shoulders. I know she knows how I feel about her. She's just being stubborn. I've been leading up to this for so long, carrying what I need in my saddle bag on my bike, because I know exactly what I want. I've been waiting for her to be sure.

I set her away from me and she looks at me curiously, but she still doesn't say anything. "I'll be right back."

I walk out to my bike and unlatch my saddlebag. Even though I'm sure she's going to say yes, I am still nervous.

When I walk into the door, she's sitting in the same spot. I walk over to her, holding her gift behind me. I bring it out and lay it on her lap. "I had this made for you."

She unfolds the black leather and holds it up. I turn it around for her and on the back it says, "Property of Bulldog."

"You got me matching jackets like Roxy and Cat?" she asks, surprised.

"Cuts. They're called cuts," I tell her.

She smiles and rubs her finger over the letters of my name. I know she's happy, but her smile still isn't reaching her face. "I love it. Thank you, Bulldog."

"You're not going to tell me how you're not my property or any other mumbo jumbo?"

She smiles wistfully. "I probably should, but no I'm not. I like being yours."

And that right there calms all my nerves.

She leans in to kiss me, but I pull back. "There's something else."

Her eyes snap to mine, but I can tell she's holding back. *Fuck, I hope she says yes.*

I pull the little box from my pocket and drop to one knee in front of her.

She gasps, her hands covering her mouth. I know she's surprised, but I fuckin' hope it's a good one.

I put my hands on her thighs because in order to do this, I have to be touching her. I have to have my hands on her. "I love you, Kate. You know I do. I love everything about you. I've never had a family, besides the Heartlands. But everything I feel when I'm with you tells me that I want to be a part of your family. I want to wake up next to you every morning and hold you in my arms at night. I want to be there for you and for Emma. I want to laugh with you, cry with you, fuck, baby, I want to do it all with you. You make me want to be a better man, and you would make me the happiest man on the planet if you would do me the honor of becoming my wife. Will you marry me, Kate?"

With tears rolling down her face, she nods her head. "Yes, oh yes. I love you, Bull. I want all of that, everything with you."

I take the ring out and put it on her finger, and it fits perfectly. She looks at it for the briefest moment and then she's in my arms, knocking me backwards to the floor with her arms around me. We're both laughing, unable to contain the high that we're both on right now.

"What's all the commotion?" Emma calls from the doorway.

Kate looks at her hand and then back to Emma, and I can tell she's searching for the right words. "Emma..."

"Did you say yes?" she asks her mom, and then turns to me. "Did she say yes?"

I nod my head at her.

"See, I told you she would say yes."

"Wait." Kate looks between Emma and me and then back to Emma. "You knew about this?"

Emma puts her hand on her hip. "Duh, he asked my permission last week, Mom. He wanted to make sure I was okay with it."

Kate smiles. "So I guess you were okay with it?"

Emma just laughs. "Yep, I agreed, as long as I could call him Pops."

"Pops!" Kate exclaims.

"Yeah," I admit. "Emma seems to think Pops is a good name for me. But I don't care. She can call me whatever. As long as I have the both of you in my life, you can even call me Oliver."

Emma starts to laugh, and when she sees that I am serious, she stops. "Wait, Oliver? Your real name is

Oliver?" She starts cracking up, holding her sides from laughing so hard.

"Har, har, Emma. Isn't it past your bedtime?" I ask her.

She turns to go, but gives us one last laugh. "Yeah, goodnight, Oliver. I mean Pops. I love you, Mom. Love you, Pops."

We can still hear her laughing as she goes down the hall, but I'm looking at the spot she just left.

Kate notices and touches my chin, to have me look at her. "Hey, you okay?"

"Yeah, but she just said she loved me."

Now it's Kate's turn to give me that "duh" look. "Of course she loves you. You've been here for her more in the past six months than her dad has in a lifetime. She loves you, Bull. I love you too."

I wipe at my eyes. Not because I'm crying or anything, but because my eyes are watering. "I love you both."

She settles back onto my lap. "I know you do."

EPILOGUE 2

KATE

Four Years Later

"You know your dad is about to have a heart attack right now. Right?" I tell Emma.

She looks over at her dad and he's surrounded by a few of the men from the Heartlands. Even from across the way, I can see his discomfort. He's used to being around people in suits and ties. I'm sure all the leather and boots are something new for him. I almost get out my phone to take a picture of him standing underneath the Ride or Die sign.

Emma just shakes her head. "Bull offered to have the party here. They closed the bar and everything. Plus, all our family is here anyway."

I have to agree with her there. If you had told me

four years ago that my family would consist of a bunch of bikers, I would have called you a liar and then laughed my head off. But looking around the bar, that's exactly what's happened.

Every one of these people have taken Emma and me in as one of their own. They've become our friends and our family.

"I can't believe you graduated high school today," I murmur, giving her a tight hug. "And my baby is going away to college."

I feel him before I hear him. Bull's arms go around Emma and me, and he holds us tight. "But college is only an hour away. I've already got it planned for Saint, Gage, and a few of the others to ride up with us when we drop her off for school."

"Pops!" Emma says, shaking her head and smiling at him. "You do know that no one will talk to me if you show up on campus glaring at everybody, right?"

"I know that no boy will, that's for sure," he deadpans right back.

She rolls her eyes, a trait she's yet to grow out of before she sees Maddox waving at her and she leaves us to go and talk to him. Bull starts to follow her, but I put my hand on his chest, reminding him, "She's eighteen now, Bull. This is her graduation party. Plus, you trust Maddox."

He looks over at his friend and gives him a *You better not think about it* glare before turning back to me. His arms go around me and he's smiling softly, and I know he's waiting on me to break down. Sort of like I have been Emma's whole senior year. "You okay, baby?"

I shrug my shoulders. "Yeah, it's going to be weird with her out of the house, but I knew this day was coming. I'm just going to miss her."

He leans down and puts his forehead to mine. "I know. Me too. Buuuuutttt...."

I give a breathless sigh. "But what?" I know Bull, and just by the look on his face, this is going to be a good one.

"Well, I tried to think about what I could do to get your mind off of Emma leaving..."

I interrupt him, rubbing my hands across shoulders. "And you're going to keep me chained to the bed for a week."

His eyes light up. "I like that idea, but no. I'm taking you to Hawaii. We're dropping Emma off at school and then we're leaving."

"Hawaii! I've always wanted to go," I say dumbly, but of course, Bull already knew that. He knows everything.

But as soon as the excitement rises, panic starts to set in. "But what if something happens? What if Emma needs me..."

He steps to the side and pulls me in front of him so I'm leaning my back against him. His arms are around me and as always, I feel more safe and loved in his arms than ever. "Look, Kate. Look at her. Do you not think that if she needs anything, our family wouldn't step in to help her?"

I look at Emma, surrounded by all the Heartlands. They're all laughing and having a good time. And I know without a doubt every one of them would be there for her if she needs it. I turn in Bull's arms and wrap my arms around his neck. "Thank you, Bull. You've given me and Emma the best life, you've shared your family with us, but most of all you've given us your love. We were lost before you came along. I love you."

He pushes the hair from my face and cups my jaw and looks into my eyes questioningly. “So, Hawaii… you good with this?”

I feel as if my heart is in my throat. “Yes. I’m good with anywhere… as long as I’m with you.”

“Me too, baby. Me too.”

HEARTLANDS

The alpha males of Heartlands Motorcycle Club are the most possessive, devoted, and territorial men in the country when it comes to the ones they love.

Heartlands is a rough and rugged new series of standalone stories. Written by four of the most trusted names in short and steamy romance, each book will get your motors revved and your hearts racing. Guaranteed.

XO, Frankie, Dani, Olivia, and Hope

CLICK HERE for the other books in the Heartlands MC Series:

FREE BOOKS

Want FREE BOOKS?

Go to www.authorhopeford.com/freebies

JOIN ME!

JOIN MY NEWSLETTER & READERS GROUP

For Up To Date Information on New Releases, Specials, and More

www.AuthorHopeFord.com/Subscribe

JOIN MY READERS GROUP ON FACEBOOK

www.FB.com/groups/hopeford

A place to talk about Hope Ford's books! Find out about new releases, giveaways, get exclusive content, see covers before anyone else and more!

Find Hope Ford at www.authorhopeford.com

ABOUT THE AUTHOR

Bestselling short romance author Hope Ford writes short, steamy, sweet romances. She loves tattooed, alpha men, instant love stories, and ALWAYS happily ever afters. She has over 60 books and they are all available on Amazon.

To find me on Pinterest, Instagram, Facebook, Goodreads, and more:

www.AuthorHopeFord.com/follow-me

Printed in Great Britain
by Amazon